FOR TOM SGOUROS

Illustrations executed in watercolor on Arches paper.
The type is Bulmer.

Clarion Books
a Houghton Mifflin Company imprint
215 Park Avenue South, New York, NY 10003
Text and illustrations copyright © 1991 by David Wiesner
All rights reserved.
For information about permission
to reproduce selections from this book, write to Permissions,
Houghton Mifflin Company, 215 Park Avenue South, New York, NY 10003.

www.hmco.com/trade

Printed in the U. S. A.

Library of Congress Cataloging-in-Publication Data
Wiesner, David.
Tuesday / written and illustrated by David Wiesner.
p.   cm.
Summary: Frogs rise on their lily pads, float through the air, and
explore nearby houses while their inhabitants sleep.
ISBN 0-395-55113-7   PA ISBN 0-395-87082-8
[1. Frogs—Fiction] I. Title.
PZ7.W6367Tu 1991   90-39358
[E]—dc20   CIP   AC

WOZ 30 29 28 27

TUESDAY

DAVID WIESNER

CLARION BOOKS
NEW YORK

TUESDAY EVENING, AROUND EIGHT.

11:21 P. M.

4:38 A.M.

NEXT TUESDAY, 7:58 P.M.